little
nye

lester

nella

gracie

Here are Little Nye and his friends.

And here

is the house

where they live.

TIME FOR A HOLIDAY
Lerryn Korda

WALKER BOOKS
AND SUBSIDIARIES
LONDON · BOSTON · SYDNEY · AUCKLAND

Summer's here
and it's hot, hot, hot!
Inside, Little Nye is
making ice lollies.

Outside, Nella has packed the big suitcase. "Time for a holiday!" she says. But the suitcase won't shut.

"Shall I take something out?" asks Lester.

He finds a ball, a kite

and a bucket and spade.

"I thought we'd play beach

games," says Nella.

But the case
still won't shut.

"Shall I take
something
else out?"
asks Gracie.

She finds a rubber ring, some flippers and a swimming mask. "We might want to go paddling and looking at fish," Nella says.

But the case still won't shut.

Little Nye comes back out,

and they all sit on top.

"What else have you got in

here?" asks Little Nye.

Nella has a long look...

"Well, I did ...

pack the dinghy..."

she says.

"... in case we sail through the spray to a faraway island."

SNAP! The suitcase clicks shut.

"Let's go!"

says Lester.

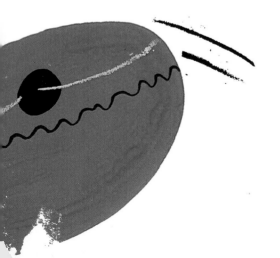

"But what about the packing?" asks Nella.

"We could have the

holiday here?"

Gracie calls.

There's sunshine, and spray

and even ice lollies!

For Katie

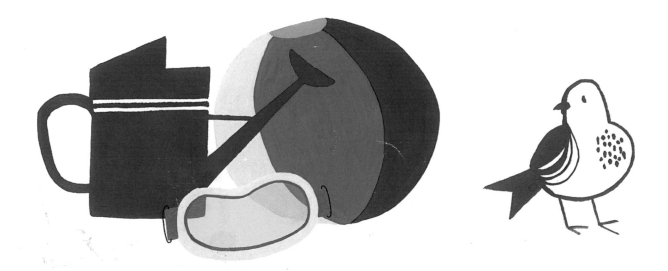

With special thanks to Ben and Lucy • First published 2010 by Walker Books Ltd, 87 Vauxhall Walk, London SE11 5HJ • 10 9 8 7 6 5 4 3 2 1
• © 2010 Lerryn Korda • The moral rights of the author-illustrator have been asserted. • This book has been typeset in Nittle Nye Medium. •
Printed in Hong Kong • All rights reserved • British Library Cataloguing in Publication Data is available. • ISBN 978-1-4063-1645-2 • **www.walker.co.uk**